THE Magic Christmas Ornament

BY JAMES BARBATO AND
VICTORIA BARBATO

Pure Imagination

There was something magical about that night. It was Christmas Eve and Victoria could hardly contain her excitement. Like so many children, she had been thinking about Christmas all year—and now it was here!

Victoria stood beneath her family's beloved Christmas tree, staring at the same ornament she had looked at a hundred times. It was her family's very favorite, very special ornament. It was the one her dad had always called "the magic Christmas ornament." Now that Victoria was seven years old, her dad had promised to tell her and her brothers the story about it.

Her parents came to sit beside the tree. Victoria and her younger brothers, Joe and John, all gathered in closely, not wanting to miss a word.

"When I was just seven years old," their father began, loosening his red, green, and gold Christmas tie, "on an icy, cold afternoon, I decided to go exploring in the woods near my house. I knew that Christmas was approaching, and I was getting restless with excitement.

"The crisp, cold forest air was calling to me, and I couldn't sit in my house any longer. So, I threw on my boots and trekked through the snow, not knowing exactly what I was looking for. But I did know that there was an enchanted feeling about the woods that day."

"Were you lost?" asked John.

"No, I was just curious. I eventually came across what looked like tiny footprints in the snow. What could they be? They looked like they could be footprints from Santa's elves. I followed the prints until they stopped right in front of a very old, mysterious tree—a grandfather tree. It was partially covered in snow and had a deep knothole beneath two arm-like branches. I thought I could see something shining inside that hole, and I leaned in closer to see what it could be."

"Were you afraid?" Joe asked.

"No, just a little cautious. I reached my hand gently into the hole and felt something round. It was a Christmas ornament, and on it was an image of a family with three kids—two boys and a girl— sitting around a Christmas tree in a cozy living room. The little boy in the picture was pointing at a glistening ornament hanging from the Christmas tree. It was the most beautiful, but curious, ornament I had ever seen. I couldn't take my eyes off it."

"Were you confused?" asked Victoria, with curiosity.

"No, I somehow knew the ornament was so magical that it had to be from Santa's own tree. I gently placed it in my pocket and went home as the sun was setting.

"Proud and pleased with my new find, I went straight to my Christmas tree and hung it on a branch right in front. I knew that I would guard this ornament for the rest of my life. And I knew that one day, when my kids were old enough, I would pass on the secret of the magic ornament."

"So, here we are. Tonight I pass the story of the ornament on to you so that you will understand the magic of Christmas lives inside of you, always, just as it lives in me."

Victoria was stunned. Could it be true? Could their very favorite, very special ornament really be magical? Was it really an ornament from Santa's own Christmas tree?

When it was time for bed, the kids could not sleep. Victoria, Joseph, and John tiptoed back downstairs to the Christmas tree. They gathered around and stared drowsily but intently at the ornament, looking for proof of the magic.

Suddenly, Joe jumped up and shouted, "Victoria! Did you see that? Something moved!"

"I see it, too!" exclaimed John.

"You're right!" said Victoria. "It looks like the picture is changing!"

Then, the ornament lit up right before their eyes. The images shifted so that when they looked at the ornament again, they could see directly into Santa's workshop!

Suddenly, the window burst open and a blast of winter air began to swirl around the room. The kids looked around, hair blowing in the wind, eyes wide in disbelief.

When they looked back at the magic ornament, they saw Santa sitting in a chair and holding a long Christmas list with their names at the top. The deeper they peered, the stronger the wind grew. Now they could see the elves working hard to make the toys in the workshop.

And then, SWOOOSH!!! The air rushed around the room. A light beamed brightly from the inside of the ornament, drawing the kids closer and closer and closer, until—

The wind settled and the kids were sitting at a table, surrounded by Santa and all of the elves. They were inside Santa's workshop!

Victoria looked at Joe and John. Their faces were flushed with shock and joy.

"Welcome, one and all!" called Santa. "Tonight is the night before Christmas. We will soon embark upon our trip around the world to deliver toys to all the girls and boys. Get ready for the most wonderful night of all!"

Victoria, Joe, and John saw stacks of toys everywhere. The boys' eyes grew big. Victoria smiled wider than she had ever smiled before. Hundreds of toy trains chugged along every surface of the workshop. A room was filled top to bottom with baby dolls. There were many shelves with little figurines that moved and danced. And—best of all—a special treasure chest brimmed with toys and sweet treats!

A young boy came and sat next to Victoria, Joseph, and John.

"Hello," he said. "My name is JJ and I would like to welcome you to the happiest place in the world . . . Santa's workshop!"

"Thank you! But how did we get here?" asked Victoria.

"Through the magic ornament, of course!" replied the boy. "Let me show you around."

JJ adjusted his tie and hopped down to the workshop floor. He had a familiar spring in his step, and he led Victoria, Joseph, and John on a tour of the happiest place in the world.

There was excitement in the air! Elves were busy wrapping last-minute gifts and decorating the most beautiful tree, which stood tall and seemed to grow bigger by the second.

"Is this Santa's Christmas tree?" asked Victoria.

"Yes, it is! Here," said JJ, as he took an ornament off the tree and tossed it to Victoria.

"Thank you," she said, almost unable to speak. She could not believe how lucky she was to have an ornament from Santa's own tree. "Wait—this looks just like the one we have on our tree at home!"

"Come on. Let me show you around outside," said JJ. He led the kids out through an enormous door and to the bordering woods. The cold, crisp air struck their cheeks as they followed closely, stepping in JJ's footprints.

They stopped right in front of a grandfather tree with a deep knothole beneath two arm-like branches. The kids glanced at each other, but did not speak a word.

Victoria proudly placed the ornament into the hole. JJ turned to the kids, smiled warmly, and said, "The spirit of Christmas lives inside of you. Always."

Suddenly, a gust of frosty snow and wind whirled around them. When it settled, the kids were back at home, warm and bewildered. The magic ornament still dangled from the Christmas tree in front of them.

The kids looked at each other and grabbed hands to ensure they were actually awake.

"Guys, guys—did you see JJ's tie!?" asked John. His voice was too excited and loud for the late hour. But the kids didn't care.

Joe's eyes glistened. He said, "I think JJ was . . ."

"I know," whispered Victoria. They didn't need to say any more. And they knew they would never forget the secrets they discovered that night. The kids had seen into the hidden world of Santa Claus. Through the story their father had passed down to them, the kids now fully understood the magic of Christmas.

Their very special, very favorite ornament continued to inspire them that Christmas, and for all the Christmases that followed.

To the love of my life, Patty, who is my strength and happiness. To my three beautiful children, Victoria, Joseph, and John, who inspire me and give me purpose. And to my wonderful, loving, and supportive family; thank you for your unconditional love. -J.B.

To my mom and dad for being the best parents, and who continue to teach us conviction, intuition, and—of course—imagination. -V.B.

Illustrations by Joe Huffman
Edited by Alli Brydon
Designed by Andrea Miller

First Edition

Library of Congress Control Number: 2019930132

ISBN (Hardback): 978-0-9998692-0-8
ISBN (eBook): 978-0-9998692-1-5
ISBN (Collection): 978-0-9998692-2-2

Pure Imagination Enterprises, LLC
www.magicchristmasbulb.com

Manufactured in the United States
10 9 8 7 6 5 4 3 2 1